I0816661

This or That?: Survival Edition

This or That

Questions About the DESERT

You Decide!

by Jaclyn Jaycox

CAPSTONE PRESS
a capstone imprint

Capstone Captivate is published by Capstone Press, an imprint of Capstone.
1710 Roe Crest Drive
North Mankato, Minnesota 56003
www.capstonepub.com

Library of Congress Cataloging-in-Publication Data
Names: Jaycox, Jaclyn, 1983– author.
Title: This or that questions about the desert / by Jaclyn Jaycox.
Description: North Mankato, Minnesota : Capstone Press, [2022] | Series: This or that? : survival edition | Includes bibliographical references and index. | Audience: Ages 8–11 | Audience: Grades 4–6 | Summary: "Would you rather be lost in the Sahara or the Gobi Desert? In this fun-filled nonfiction title, young adventurers will face decisions about surviving in a sandy wasteland. Readers will sharpen their decision-making skills with more than a dozen thought-provoking questions about deserts. From scary to gross to just plain silly, this book generates discussion and promotes critical-thinking skills. Full-color photographs and engaging easy-to-read facts invite readers to make informed decisions while also prompting further research"—Provided by publisher.
Identifiers: LCCN 2021006156 (print) | LCCN 2021006157 (ebook) | ISBN 9781663907035 (hardcover) | ISBN 9781663907004 (pdf) | ISBN 9781663907028 (kindle edition)
Subjects: LCSH: Desert survival—Juvenile literature.
Classification: LCC GV200.5 .J39 2022 (print) | LCC GV200.5 (ebook) | DDC 613.6/9—dc23
LC record available at https://lccn.loc.gov/2021006156
LC ebook record available at https://lccn.loc.gov/2021006157

Image Credits
Shutterstock: Alexandra Lande, Cover (camel), Anton Petrus, 26, apstockphoto, 3, arka38, Cover (cactus), David ODell, 7, Dmitry Niko, 10, Homo Cosmicos, 24, JAlmon73, 9, Jiri Prochazka, 8, John D Sirlin, Cover (dust storm), Joshua Resnick, 21, Ket4up, Cover (sun), Kirill Trifonov, 4, Kris Wiktor, 15, Lucky-photographer, 23, Mattia Mazzucchelli, 28, Mike Hardiman, 11, Mikhail Gnatkovskiy, 13, Nimit Virdi, 16, Oleg Kovtun Hydrobio, 14, rontav, 17, Roop_Dey, 19, Sahara Prince, 6, Symbiosis Australia, 29, Tomacrosse, 27, tr3gin, 18, travelview, 22, Vinte Vintage, 20, Winston Springwater, 13, Wojciech Dziados, 25

Design Element: Shutterstock: Morphart Creation, Cover (map)

Editorial Credits
Editor: Gena Chester; Designer: Heidi Thompson; Media Researcher: Jo Miller; Production Specialist: Tori Abraham

Words in **bold** are in the glossary.

Printed in the United States 4828

About the Desert

Deserts are some of the hottest and driest places in the world. But did you know they can also be cold? Deserts are found on every continent. They cover about one-fifth of Earth. Deserts are places that receive less than 10 inches (25 centimeters) of rain or snow every year.

Desert weather can be extremely harsh. But the desert **biome** is an important part of Earth. Some plants and animals that live in deserts aren't found anywhere else. Many people also live there. In fact, about 1 billion people call deserts home.

How to Use This Book

Imagine you are on a journey to explore a desert. Which one would you visit? What would you do? Watch out! The desert can be a dangerous place.

Read on to find questions about surviving in the desert. The questions are followed by information to help you make your decisions. Choose one or the other. Just be sure to weigh your options carefully! Your life could depend on it.

Would You Choose **This**

visit the desert during the day

In most hot deserts, daytime temperatures can average more than 100 degrees Fahrenheit (38 degrees Celsius). The sun beating down on you causes your body to heat up. Sweating can cause dehydration. You must have lots of drinking water with you! Finding shade to cool off can be tough. In some deserts, cacti, bushes, and large rocks are few and far between.

Deserts can get very cold after the sun goes down. Temperatures in hot deserts can drop to below freezing at night. If you don't have warm clothing, your body temperature will drop. This can lead to hypothermia. But the desert comes alive at night! Many desert animals are **nocturnal**. You might see tarantulas, bobcats, or snakes.

What do you do if you are stuck in the desert without food? Try eating a scorpion! These creatures are packed with protein. Be careful catching them, though. They can sting! You can eat them raw. But you must remove their stinger and venom first. Or you can roast them over a fire. Some people say a cooked scorpion tastes like chicken.

OR

That? eat a stink bug

Just as their name suggests, stink bugs are stinky! But in a pinch, they can make a good meal. Like scorpions, they are a great source of protein. They are also easy to catch. You can soak and then cook them to get rid of their smell. You can also eat them raw. Some people say they taste like apples.

Would You Choose

This

get stuck in a sandstorm

- ✓ can happen suddenly
- ✓ easy to get lost
- ✓ risk of eye irritation, cough, and breathing problems

Desert sandstorms usually happen in the summer. Strong winds pick up dry sand and dirt. They can come out of nowhere and catch you off guard. There is a risk of sand getting in your eyes, nose, mouth, and lungs. This can cause eye irritation, coughing, and breathing problems.

OR That? get stuck in a flash flood

- ✓ happens quickly
- ✓ risk of injury or being carried away by fast-flowing water
- ✓ risk of death

The desert ground is dry and hard. When it rains, the water doesn't soak into the ground. Flash floods happen quickly. They are one of the biggest causes of death in the desert. These fast-flowing waters can knock you off your feet. They carry lots of **debris**, including huge rocks!

Would You Choose

This

take emergency shelter in a cave

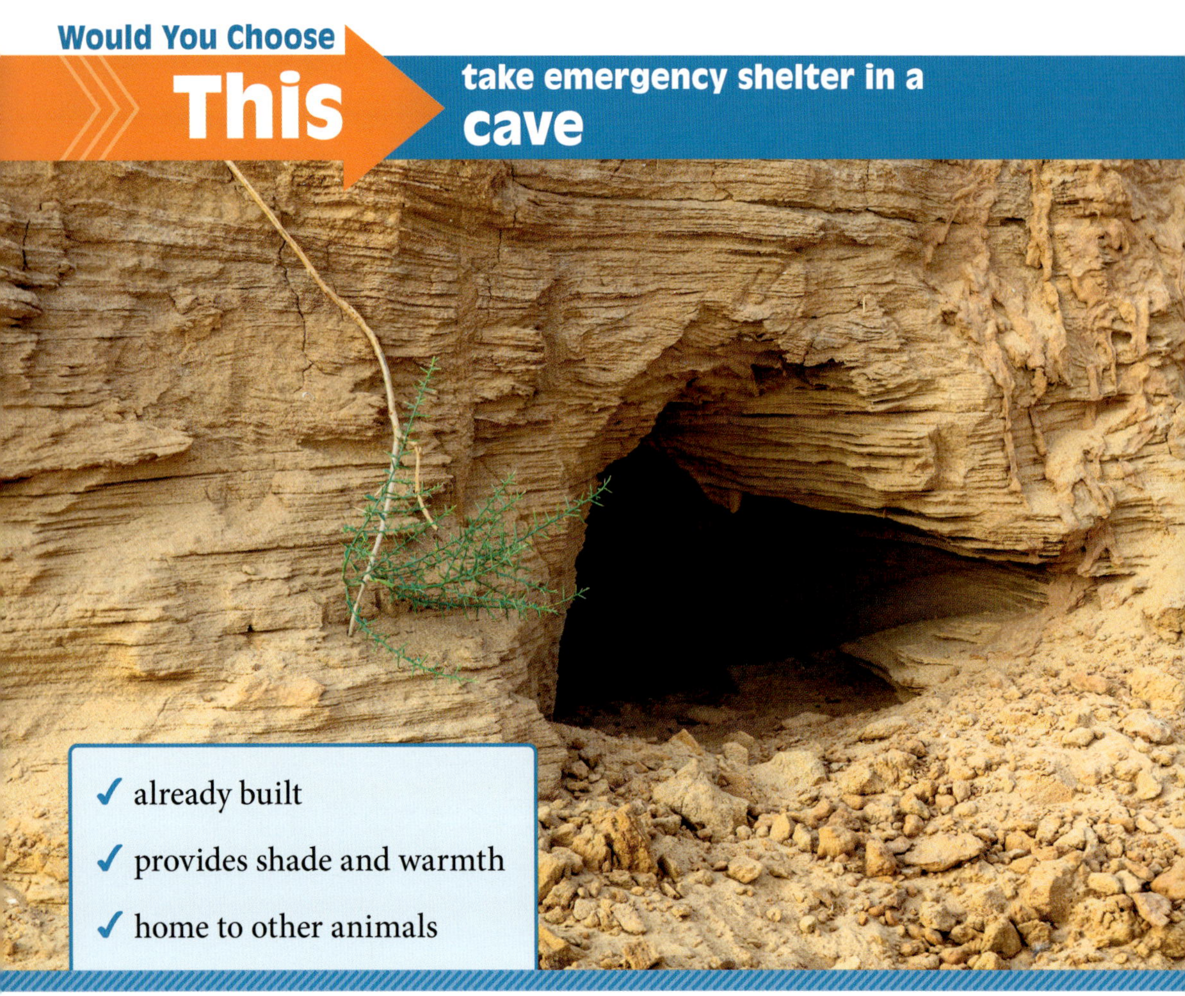

✓ already built

✓ provides shade and warmth

✓ home to other animals

If you are stranded in the desert, you will need to find shelter. You could look for a cave. A cave can provide shade during the day and warmth at night. If you are lucky enough to find one, beware. Snakes, scorpions, and bobcats also make their homes there!

OR

That? take emergency shelter in a makeshift cocoon

✓ make it yourself

✓ protects you from the sun

✓ much cooler underground

Some desert areas are just sand as far as the eye can see. You could build yourself a makeshift **cocoon**. Dig a deep trench in the sand the size of your body. Cover it with a blanket or tarp. Crawl inside to escape the desert heat. It can be as much as 40°F (22°C) cooler in the ground than on top of it.

You've run out of water.
Would You Choose

This try to find some

- risk of dehydration
- water sources are scarce
- risk of sickness

Any activity in extreme heat will make you sweat. Searching for water while it's hot can cause dehydration to set in faster. Water sources can be tough to find in the desert. It is possible to get water from a cactus. But don't drink more than a few sips! Too much can make you very sick.

OR

That? stay put

✓ 3–4 days to live

✓ lose less body water

✓ wait to be rescued

A person can survive about three to four days without water. You could focus on staying in a shelter and trying to keep cool. This helps avoid losing water from sweating. But you will have limited time to be rescued. Making a fire at night or drawing a large X on the ground can help airplanes spot you.

Would You Choose **This** come across a saw-scaled viper

✓ aggressive

✓ venomous

✓ risk of severe injury or death

Saw-scaled vipers are one of many kinds of snakes found in the desert. They are small and aggressive. They will bite if you get too close! These snakes are extremely venomous. In areas where they are found, they've caused more human deaths than all other kinds of snakes combined. Even people who have survived have lost fingers or limbs.

Ostriches are found in Africa. They can't fly, but they are quick on their feet! Ostriches can run up to 45 miles (72 kilometers) per hour. They can be aggressive, especially if they are protecting their eggs. They may try to chase **predators** away. Or they will use their strong legs to attack. A kick from an ostrich can kill predators like lions, and even humans!

Riding in a **dune** buggy can be a fun way to explore the desert. This vehicle can make traveling over large sand dunes easy. It can go as fast as a car. But traveling at high speeds on rough desert **terrain** can also be dangerous. A buggy can tip over or roll. Crashes can seriously injure the driver and passengers.

People have been traveling through deserts on camels for thousands of years. Camels can last up to seven months without drinking water. They can carry up to 1,300 pounds (590 kilograms). But they usually only travel about 25 miles (40 km) a day. The slower travel will keep you in the desert longer. You will need to be prepared with plenty of supplies!

Would You Choose This a first aid kit

- ✓ injuries are likely in the desert
- ✓ able to clean wounds
- ✓ extra weight to carry

Like everywhere else, injuries can happen in the desert. Many desert plants have thorns that can cut through skin. There are stinging creatures, such as scorpions or wasps. Cuts or stings can quickly become infected. With a first aid kit, you can clean and cover wounds. But you may not need everything inside. And carrying the extra weight can work against you.

OR

That? five gallons of water

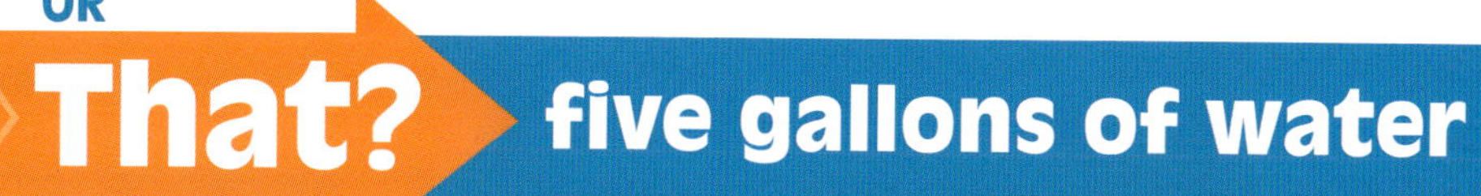

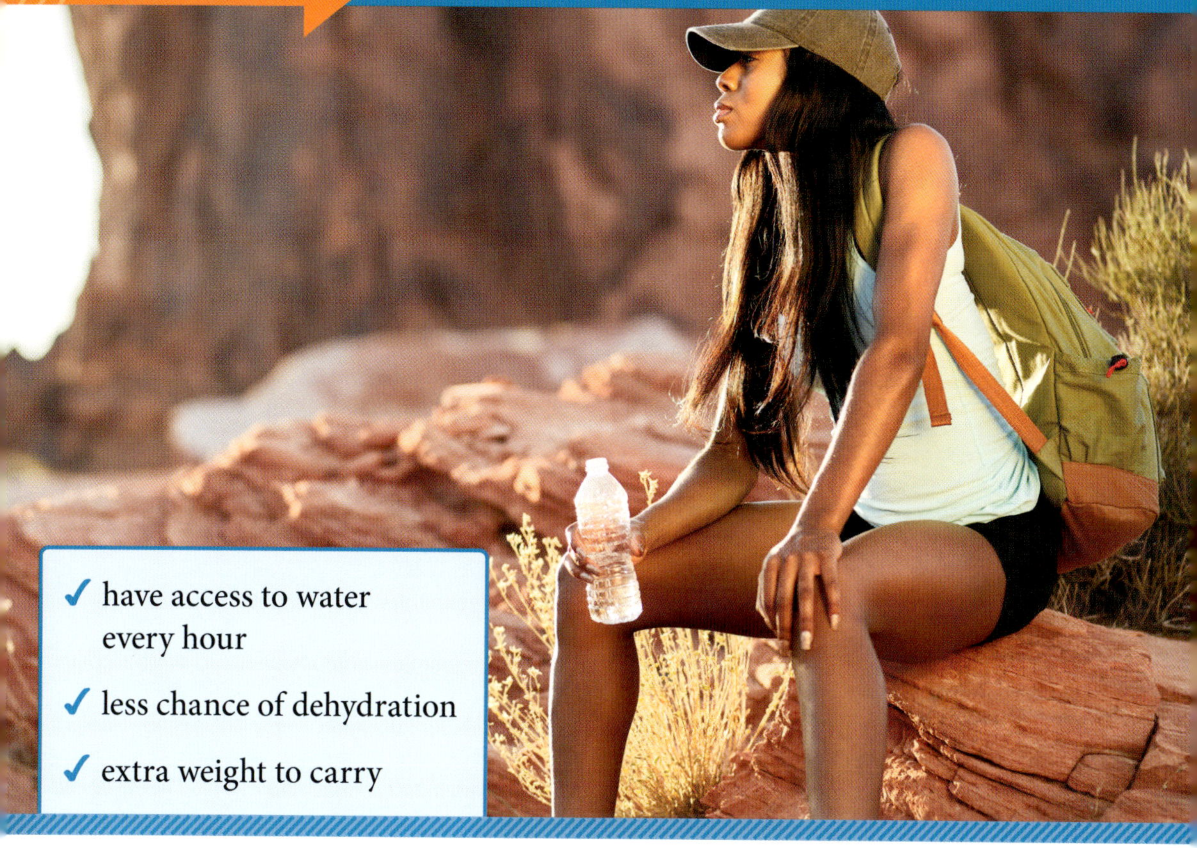

- ✓ have access to water every hour
- ✓ less chance of dehydration
- ✓ extra weight to carry

Water is very important in the desert. Experts recommend to take a drink of water at least once every hour. While hiking in the heat, a person can losc about 0.5 gallon (2 liters) of water per hour from sweating. But carrying 5 gallons (19 L) by yourself is a lot of work! Each gallon weighs about 8 pounds (4 kg).

Would You Choose

This

suffer from heatstroke

- ✓ causes headache, dizziness, and vomiting
- ✓ must find shade immediately
- ✓ can lead to unconsciousness and death

Heatstroke is an extreme loss of water and salt from the body. The body is not able to cool itself off. Lack of sweat, headache, and dizziness are all signs of heatstroke. Vomiting and increased heart rate can happen too. This serious condition can lead to unconsciousness and even death. So it is critical to get help and find shade to cool down as soon as possible.

OR

That? suffer from valley fever

- ✓ risk of death
- ✓ infection may take months to go away
- ✓ potentially no symptoms

Valley fever occurs in deserts in the southwestern U.S., Central America, and South America. It's an infection caused by inhaling **fungi** that live in the dirt. Some people who breathe in this fungus don't get sick. But those who do can have a cough, shortness of breath, and rash. It usually goes away after a few weeks or months. In rare cases, it can be deadly.

Would You Choose This: visit the Sahara

The Sahara is found in northern Africa. It is the largest hot desert in the world. The continental United States could fit inside it! Temperatures in the Sahara can reach a dangerous 122°F (50°C). Sandstorms are common and can happen suddenly. Blowing sand makes it hard to see. You can easily become lost.

OR That? visit Antarctica

- ✓ largest cold desert
- ✓ extremely cold temperatures
- ✓ blizzards are common

Antarctica is the largest cold desert in the world. It is one of the driest and windiest places on Earth. It gets very little snowfall each year. Winter temperatures can reach –128°F (–89°C). Blizzards happen suddenly and often in Antarctica. Getting lost in a blizzard in the extreme cold can be deadly.

Would You Choose This visit the Gobi Desert

- ✓ largest desert in Asia
- ✓ extremely cold winter temperatures
- ✓ very little water

The Gobi Desert is the largest desert in Asia. It has hot summers and very cold winters. Winter temperatures can reach −40°F (−40°C). Warm clothes and shelter are a must to survive the freezing cold. The Himalayan Mountains block rain clouds from reaching the desert. Water can be almost impossible to find.

OR

That? visit the Atacama Desert

- ✓ driest nonpolar desert in the world
- ✓ risk of flooding
- ✓ similar to going to Mars

The Atacama Desert in South America is the driest desert in the world outside of the polar regions. Scientists compare some of the conditions here to Mars. The ground is hard and dry. This causes major flooding when it rains. Many people have died in these floods.

Would You Choose

This

stay with your broken-down car

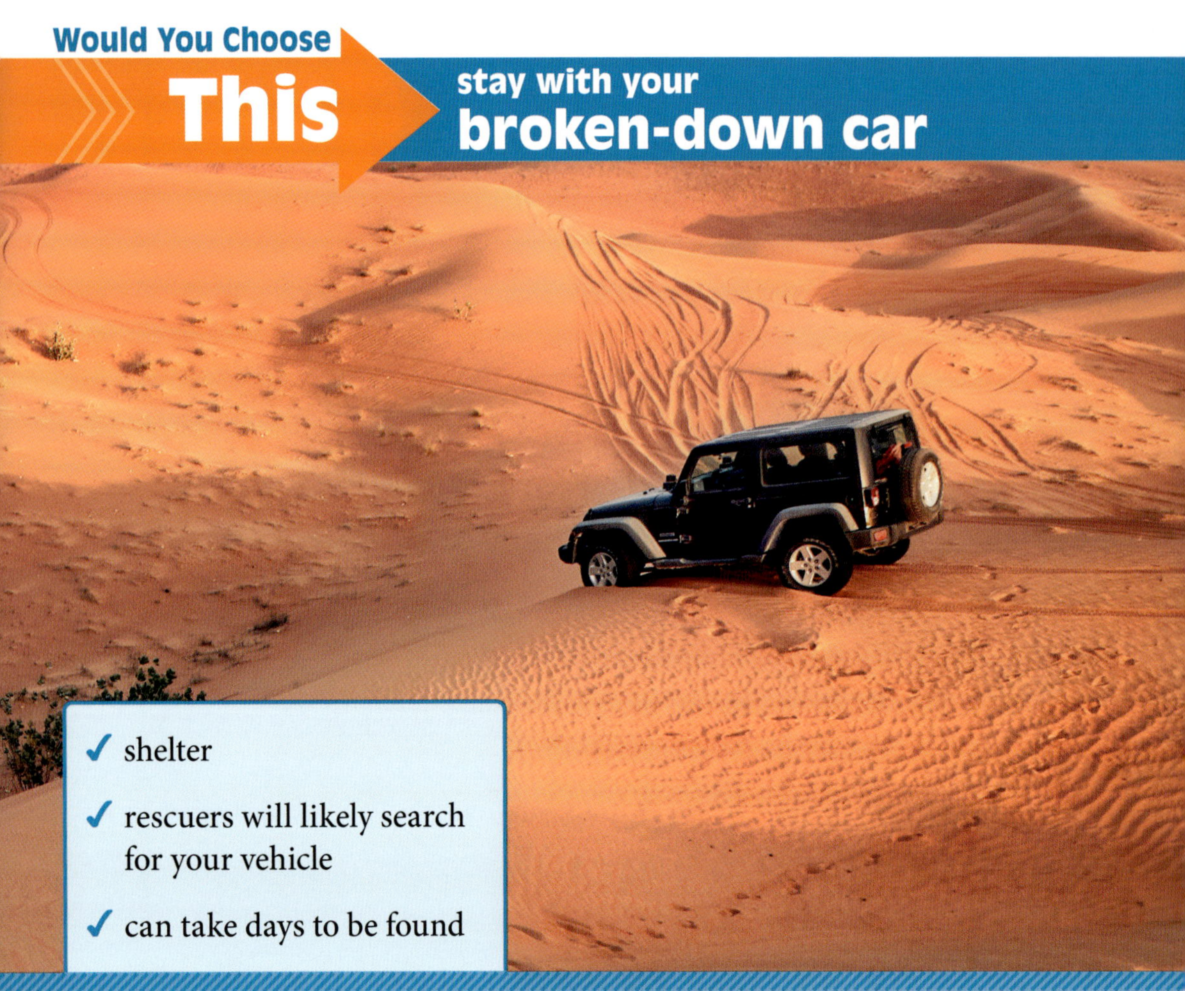

- ✓ shelter
- ✓ rescuers will likely search for your vehicle
- ✓ can take days to be found

Staying with your car if it breaks down in the desert provides shelter. You might have a blanket in your car to make yourself shade outside. If you are stuck overnight, staying in your car could keep you warm. If someone has reported you missing, rescuers will likely be searching for your vehicle. But if you are far from a road, it could take them days to find you.

OR

That? go search for help

✓ may be found sooner

✓ risk of getting lost

✓ no protection from animals

Searching for help might be best if you are not near a well-traveled road. You could pop the car hood open and leave a note saying where you are headed. If any passersby stop, they will know where to look for you. But there are risks. You could get lost. You would have no protection from wild animals. Or you could encounter any of the other countless dangers found in this harsh biome.

Lightning Round

Would you choose to . . .

- take your dog **or** go alone?
- have your cell phone **or** a printed map?
- come across a coyote **or** a cougar?
- have a hat **or** sunscreen?
- hike up a desert mountain **or** down into a canyon?
- have a whistle **or** a flare gun?
- ration your water **or** drink it when you're thirsty?

Glossary

biome (BY-ohm)—an area with a particular type of climate and certain plants and animals that live there

cocoon (kuh-KOON)—a type of shelter for one person

debris (DUH-bree)—pieces of something that has been broken apart

dehydration (dee-hy-DRAY-shuhn)—a life-threatening medical condition caused by a lack of water

dune (DOON)—a hill or ridge of sand piled up by wind

fungus (FUHN-guhs)—a living thing similar to a plant, but without flowers, leaves, or green coloring

hypothermia (hy-po-THUR-mee-uh)—a life-threatening condition that happens when a person's temperature is too low and the body is losing heat faster than it can produce it

nocturnal (nok-TUR-nuhl)—active at night and at rest during the day

predator (PRED-uh-tur)—an animal that hunts other animals for food

protein (PRO-teen)—a substance found in foods that is an important part of the human diet

terrain (tuh-RAYN)—the surface of the land

venom (VEN-uhm)—a poisonous liquid produced by some animals; a venomous animal produces venom

Read More

Clark, Ginjer L. *Life in the Gobi Desert.* New York: Penguin Random House, 2018.

Eboch, M. M. *Desert Biomes Around the World.* North Mankato, MN: Capstone Press, 2020.

Johnson, Rebecca L. *A Walk in the Desert.* Minneapolis: Lerner Publications, 2021.

Internet Sites

DK Find Out!: Deserts
dkfindout.com/us/earth/deserts/

Kiddle: Desert Facts for Kids
kids.kiddle.co/Desert

National Geographic Kids: Desert Habitat
kids.nationalgeographic.com/explore/nature/habitats/desert/